Thirty and single? Well, getcha ass to the Gathering!

As if hitting thirty wasn't enough, unmated Scarlet Wickham is summoned to this year's Gathering. As a woman Marked to be the mate of an Alpha pair, she's not going to find happiness anywhere other than in the arms of two Alpha werewolves. So, off she goes with her sisters in tow. 'Cause yeah, she's one of the plump Wickham triplets, and they're all being carted off to werewolf speed dating.

Keller and Madden, Ruling Alpha pair, can't believe their luck. They've found their mate, and she's more than they could have ever hoped for. She's feisty with spirit to spare, and lush curves that they want to trace with their tongues. They can't wait to solidify their bond and get to know the beautiful woman who is to rule at their side. But first, there's the minor inconvenience of a challenge to the death…

# CHAPTER ONE

The damned thing wouldn't burn. Scarlet had tried. Twice.

The invitation had appeared bright and early, popping onto her counter the moment the clock had struck 8:01 A.M. and she'd officially hit thirty.

Unmated and thirty.

Fuuuccckkk.

She glared at the pristine page, at the cream linen that boasted the handwritten words requesting her attendance at the coming Gathering.

Request. Right.

She glanced at her scorched sink, frowned and wondered if steel polish would remove the marks. That thought brought her back to the idea of burning the invite and she wondered if the local witch could help her out. Maybe...

The shrill ring of her phone busted in on her illegal wonderings. If she were honest, which she didn't want to be, she had already broken the law by attempting to burn the stupid paper. Having a Mark meant she had to adhere to the same rules that governed the furballs. So, no circumventing a wolfy summons. Even if she wasn't a wolf.

With a sigh, she abandoned her spot at the counter and snatched up the phone. Holding the handset between her cheek and shoulder she greeted her caller. "Heya."

1

The caller screamed. Scarlet took a peek at the microwave clock. 8:14 A.M.

"So, you got your invite." She smirked, kind of glad she wouldn't be the only one forcefully attending the upcoming annual Gathering.

Scarlet was one of three, the first-born of the Wickham fraternal triplets. Each of them as different from the other as the stars in the sky. Thankfully, it'd only be her and Gabriella attending. The third, Whitney, had been born sans the necessary birthmark, so she wouldn't be receiving the mandatory summons. Lucky bitch.

"They can't do this!"

Scarlet eased her ear from the handset. "Apparently, they can."

She wanted to say "duh", but refrained. They should have been prepared for this, should have had some sort of plan. Like, Operation: What the Fuck to do When Forced to Parade Ourselves in Front of Mate Hunting Wolves When We Hit Thirty. Instead, Scarlet had pushed the eventuality from her mind, conveniently forgetting that particular law. Apparently, Gabby had done the same.

She fingered the unmarred invitation. "I'm pretty sure Mom covered all this during the whole 'What to Expect When You're Marked' lessons."

"Quit being rational and logical," her sister snapped. "I'm too busy for this, Scarlet. You need to do something. Go…do what you do." She imagined Gabby waving her hands around, fingers fluttering, and she smiled. Her sister in a tizzy was something to watch.

Her mongrel cat Burger came sneaking over and twined around her ankles. While listening to her sister rant and rave at the injustice of their summoning, she fed her sweet boy. Scraping out the rest of his organic, homemade cat food, she stood and placed the empty container in the sink. She'd have to make him more food for the pet sitter before she flew out to the Gathering. Mentally, she ticked through the contents of her freezer. He tended to like the shrimp and salmon more than—

"Are you even listening to me?" Gabby's screech nearly blew her eardrum.

"Not really." She stared down at Burger. "Do you think I'll have to get rid of my cat?"

The thought poked at her heart and deflated it. She'd rescued him when she first graduated from college. It'd been her and Burger against the world.

"Scarlet!" She heard her sister panting and gasping with rage.

"What? I mean, Burger's a cat, they're wolves. I don't want them eating him." Silence met her. "Just sayin'."

Scarlet understood Gabby's feelings, sensed her sister near the edge of sanity, and there wasn't a damn thing she could do about the situation. She was as freaked-the-fuck-out over the slip of paper as her sister, but she dealt with things with humor. Humor few people appreciated.

They'd both been born with a Mark, a symbol of their inevitable mating to Alpha wolves.

And it'd be Alphas. Plural. Not because they'd meet more than one wolf. No, because they'd be *mating* more than one wolf. Alphas ruled in pairs, the men sometimes related, generally not. But there were always two.

Women in the Wickham line had been partnering with the furballs for as long as they could remember, though not necessarily every generation. Their mother hadn't been Marked and had happily settled with a lovely human man. But two out of the three triplets had been born with the three-pointed, spiraling symbol. Looking more like a scar than anything else, the Mark was slightly raised and a hint darker than her natural skin tone.

So she and Gabby would be mating a pair of wolves. Subconsciously, she'd been waiting for the invite. Once a Marked woman hit thirty and was still unmated, the Ruling Alphas summoned the ladies to the annual Gathering to meet Alphas from outside the female's hometown.

Basically, werewolf speed dating.

Sniff-sniff. Am I your mate? No? Next!

The Alpha pairing could form at any time. Once one wolf recognized a power that matched his own in another wolf, they bonded. From there they either formed a new pack or took over another. She was sure there was more secret furball mumbo jumbo involved, but that was the extent of her non-mated knowledge. Oh, she'd asked, and her mother had said: "You'll find out when you're mated, dear."

Great.

The problems with Alpha pairs arose from the fact that both were controlling and dominant as hell. Which is where the Marked came in. The ladies acted as the balance, the one who kept the two calm. Sure, the guys could rule without

4

one; the world was just better if they had a mate at their side. Less bloody, too.

She took a deep breath. She'd have to travel and meet some wolves. If she found her Alphas, group sex would occur, one male in her pussy and the other in her ass, some scar-inducing biting, and voila, mates. She'd never had sex with two men at once. So, yeah, that was scary as hell. But then again, two men pleasuring her at the same time had…possibilities.

"Scarlet? I don't think I can keep two men happy." A sniffle reached her.

"Oh, honey." She sighed. Poor Gabby. She'd been through hell the past few years. She'd been dating, regardless of the fact that she was Marked, and had fallen in love several times. Only the men had torn her heart to shreds and left a broken Gabriella in their wake. "You know none of that is your fault. It's theirs. We've talked about this."

Another sniffle. "But Allen said—"

"No. Allen said a lot of things. He also put his dick in other women. His cheating had nothing to do with you." Part of her wished she were a wolf. Then she could have gone and torn that sorry excuse for a man apart. "Good sex takes two people, and Gabby, I've seen you on the dance floor. Your crappy sex life is so not your fault. Hips don't lie."

"I know, it's just—"

A low beep interrupted her sister and Scarlet glanced at the caller ID. Whitney. "Hold on a sec."

Her gaze shot to the microwave clock. 8:36 A.M.

5

Scarlet flashed over to her other sister. "Whit?"

"It's a mistake. Scarlet, it has to be. Has to." She heard the tears in her sister's voice, the heartbreak that filled every word. "Why are they doing this to me? I'm not Marked, Scarlet. Isn't that enough? I finally got over not having the stupid Mark and now they're messing with me like this?" Whitney sobbed.

"You got an invitation? From the Ruling Alphas?"

"Yes." Her poor sister was such a sensitive soul.

Anger bubbled in her chest, churned and grew until she felt as if she'd explode beneath the feelings coursing through her veins. Scarlet and Gabby had always viewed the Marks as a sort of death sentence, seeing them as something that stole their free will. Finding a mate was biological and had nothing to do with emotions. No gentle "getting to know each other" period like with human men. Relationships between a Marked and wolves were more along the lines of: *You're our mate. Bend over. We mate you now.* That'd be followed by a grunt.

At least, that's what she'd gotten from her mother's explanations. Scarlet and Gabriella had agreed that they'd put off mating as long as possible. The wolves that claimed them could be total assholes, and they'd be stuck with them for life. They'd decided to enjoy a little freedom before the ax finally fell. And then they'd sort of forgotten about the whole Gathering thing. *Oops.*

Geez, even when she'd adopted her cat from the shelter, she'd gotten a trial run.

6

Go to a Gathering voluntarily? Nu uh. Over their dead bodies.

The only one who'd craved a Mark was Whitney. Sweet, delicate Whitney. From the moment they began playing dress-up, Whit was the gorgeous bride who married not one, but two men. Two werewolves. She just didn't carry a Mark.

And through a weird twist of nature, Alpha wolves didn't mate with human women unless there was a Mark. Single, non-Alphas only mated female furballs. It was two for a human or nada. It had something to do with the way a girl wolf interacted with two boy wolves and yada, yada… She'd sort of tuned her mom's voice out after that.

"Scarlet?"

"Shh… It's okay. We'll figure it out. If it's a mistake, I'll beat the shit out of the Ruling Alphas for upsetting you." She would. Without a doubt. "If—" She licked her lips, mouth dry. "If they've somehow changed things, we'll find you the best set of furries out there." Scarlet took a deep breath. "Or, we can try and hide you. Whatever you decide, Whit."

Her sister sniffled. "It says I have to go. *Have to.* There's punishments and stuff." Just like there were punishments for exposing werewolves to the general public, there were consequences for refusing an order from the Ruling Alphas.

Scarlet sighed, ran a hand over her face and pinched the bridge of her nose. "I hadn't read that far yet. I sort of tried burning it once I got past the first line." Whitney giggled. "The damn things found us, so there is probably a lovely bunch of witches involved in the whole thing. Which means that if we don't show, the punishment will probably kick in." Scarlet swallowed past the lump in her throat. "So, yeah, we gotta go. But I'll take care of you Whitney. No matter what, nothing is gonna happen that you don't want. I promise."

She stroked her cat, taking comfort in his gentle purr. "Okay, I've got Gabby on the other line. Lemme do a three-way call, and we can make plans. We're going to the damned Gathering whether we like it or not, so we might as well go all-out."

# CHAPTER TWO

If Scarlet had known wolves were chock full-o-hotness, she would have hunted them up long ago. Or, at least, she wouldn't have been so cranky about attending the Gathering. Yum.

With her sisters huddled against her back, she led them through the growing throng. Male wolves meandered amongst the women, and she saw more than one set of Alphas lean toward a female for a discreet sniff. Based on what she'd been told at check-in, their "conference" consisted of four thousand attendees from around the world. That was a lot of Marked chicks and Alpha pairs.

One such pair stepped into her path and blocked their passage. She glared at the men. Both were large, well over six feet, gorgeous…and in her way.

"Excuse me." She stepped to the right, only to have her path obstructed once again. She gritted her teeth and smiled. "Excuse me, I'd like to get by. I have to speak to the Ruling Alphas."

"Well, we need to see if any of you belong to us. All of the Marked must submit—"

Oh, so the wrong thing to say. Her sisters had been giving themselves pep talks from the moment their plane left Atlanta. No letting Alphas walk all over them.

"Submit? Belong to you?" Gabby's voice was way too quiet. She stepped up and stood beside Scarlet. "You want to know if one of us belongs to you, that it?"

"Gabriella..." Her sister's voice had taken on the brittle tone she knew all too well. It usually came right before...

Gabby kept on going. "Should I bend over so you can sniff my ass? That's what dogs do, right?" The man's face turned a blazing shade of red. Alphas, as a rule, didn't like people talking back to them. It was a control thing.

"If you were my bitch—"

Scarlet waited to see if the vein in the wolf's temple popped. That'd be fun.

"If I was your *bitch*, I'd carve the Mark from my flesh and fuck the consequences. Listen, asshole, I'm here because I don't have a choice. So, *fuck* and *you*." Gabby spat the words at the giant wolf. The giant wolf who looked about ready to tear her limb from limb.

"Is there a problem?" The most seductive velvet voice overrode her sister's next words, and Scarlet suddenly felt the need to melt into the floor. A heavy wave of dominance far superior to that of the men they'd been arguing with, blanketed her. This guy was definitely stronger than the other two men. Dominance came on a sort of sliding scale, some wolves more powerful than others. This speaker was seriously dominant, and it made her wonder what it'd feel like to be in the Ruling Alphas' presence. Their strength would probably drop her to her knees.

She turned her focus to the newcomer. Scratch that, *newcomers*. If she'd been a cat, she would have rubbed against them and begged for their touch.

While his companion was bulky, the man who'd spoken was tall and lithe. He had the body of a swimmer, accentuated by lean limbs that appeared to pulse with strength. Power surrounded him like a hidden shroud, and the jerk they'd been arguing with immediately fell silent. She let her gaze travel over the wolf, noting the pale brown hair with a hint of a curl, his long lashes and hazel eyes. His patrician nose had a bump along the ridge, attesting to a past break. His lips looked insanely kissable, yet furrowed lines surrounded them. The man frowned entirely too much. Like now.

"Garron?" He focused on the jerk who'd been giving them a hard time. "Quentin?" His attention went to the other wolf.

"Of course not, Alpha." Garron, or "Asshole" in Scarlet's mind, tilted his head. Showing deference to the new wolf, as well as exposing his own neck, confirmed Scarlet's suspicions. The sexy wolf was definitely more dominant than Asshole. "We simply requested that these Marked submit, per the law of the Gathering."

Scarlet seethed. First, at his wording and second, because the man didn't know what the hell he was talking about. No idiot should try quoting the laws when he couldn't tell his asshole from a hole in the ground.

When the powerful Alpha opened his mouth, Scarlet cut him off. "Alpha, if I may?"

That drew the attention of his companion, the larger presence she'd been trying to ignore. Where the first Alpha was lean, this one was built like a tank. Hell, his neck was nearly as thick as her thigh and her thighs weren't small. But those eyes… Those sparkling blue eyes lured her. They called to her and beckoned her a little closer. She leaned toward him. What would it be like to—

"Of course, Miss…" The first Alpha let the word trail off, and she filled in the blanks.

"Wickham. Scarlet Wickham." She shook her head to clear the burgeoning arousal from her mind and focused on the less dominant wolf, Garron, ignoring the asshole's partner, Quentin. "It's your belief that the Marked who attend the Gathering must submit upon your demand? That is your understanding of the laws?"

Gabby had learned all of the laws. Every. Single. One. And had then drilled them into her and Whitney's brains. Her sister figured if they were gonna be forced into the dog (heh) and pony show, they needed to be as knowledgeable as possible. Plus, Gabs had been hunting for a loophole. Scarlet had simply paid attention long enough to get the gist of things. Of course, it'd probably come back to bite her on the ass. Much like tuning out her mother had done with the whole "forgetting about the Gathering" thing.

Garron snorted. "Of course I know the law. I—"

"It's not your turn to speak, Garron." The Alpha quieted the man, and her attraction to him and his partner increased.

She was suddenly not quite so pissed about being summoned. Her Mark tingled, heating and pricking right below her right shoulder.

Her mates were near. Not the two guys who'd blocked them. The new Alphas? Regardless, she'd found her mates.

12

Portions of her raged against fate. She'd have to uproot her life. Move. And there was the fact that they could be total dicks. Who was to say they wouldn't be like Garron and Quentin? They could treat her like shit.

Unfortunately, her other half, the bit that'd been lonely, rejoiced.

She had a guy to smack down first.

"Miss Wickham?" The hazel-eyed devil raised a single eyebrow.

The puny asshole, Garron rolled his eyes. She ignored him. "I'm assuming you know the first law. That a Marked shall never be harmed. Now, the second addresses a Marked's submission."

"See? You must—" A half-shifted claw wrapped around Garron's throat. Way to go, badass Alpha.

"The first clause of the second law does say that each Marked must submit to the Test of Proximity."

A gurgling gasp came from Garron, and the Alpha turned to her with a wide, toothy smile. "Continue Miss Wickham."

"The law governing the Test of Proximity indicates it is the Marked who initiates and concludes the test. An Alpha pair may request the test, but, outside arranged Gatherings, no Marked is *required* to submit." She glanced back at her sisters. "I didn't agree to anything, did you?" Both Gabby and Whitney shook their heads, wide smiles in place. "So, my sisters didn't agree to the Test of Proximity. I didn't agree to the Test of Proximity, and I know for damned sure this is time set aside for registration. Thus, no required submission."

She tilted her head to the side. "In fact, I do happen to recall that direct violation of Gathering laws in relation to the Marked, and their treatment, results in immediate expulsion. The laws are in place for *our* protection, not so you can come in and be a dictator. We are balance. We are your cherished. We sure as hell aren't here to get barked at and sniffed."

Garron's reddening face paled, and the other wolf, Quentin, growled low. Apparently the other half of Garron's pair didn't care for what he heard. Well, she didn't like being around assholes, so they were even.

The stocky man tensed, hands flexing and then they became claws. A rolling growl overrode Quentin's, and the wolf quickly quieted.

"Thank you, Madden." The lean Alpha's voice was calm, smooth and not hinting at the tiniest bit of stress from holding Garron still. "Miss Wickham is correct. She asked you to move. Twice. You made demands of her and her..." He glanced at her, eyebrow raised in a silent question.

"Sisters."

"You made demands of the Sisters Wickham." The unknown Alpha pushed Garron away and, for the first time, Scarlet noticed the guards surrounding them. "Have this Alpha pair escorted from the grounds."

Way to make an entrance.

Snarls and growls filled the air as the two asshole Alphas were drawn from the area, the guards doing their jobs as

14

ordered. Which left Scarlet and her sisters with a thinning crowd and two massive, fuck-me-now Alphas.

"Um, thank you?"

The leaner of the two smiled, a slight quirk of his lips. "I'm sorry it was necessary. Unmated Alphas can come on a little strong and push the laws a little, but those two are too aggressive to remain. Apologies." He bowed ever so slightly, bringing him nearer, and it took everything in her not to reach out and run her fingers through those slight curls. "I'm Alpha Keller Aaron, and this is my partner Alpha Madden Harris."

Gabriella gasped, but Scarlet ignored her sister. She was too interested in the gorgeous men before her.

Keller continued. "We welcome you to the Gathering. If there's any assistance we can provide, please don't hesitate to ask."

Keller glanced at Madden, and their gazes remained locked as if they fought in a silent battle. Finally, Alpha Keller's attention returned to her. "At this time, if you are amenable, we would like engage in a Test of Proximity."

Scarlet blinked. Then blinked again before turning her head to look at Gabby. "Do you want to go with them?"

Her sister's expression went from a mixture of wide-eyed fear and surprise to completely blank and devoid of emotion. She'd have to ask Gabby about that later. "They don't want me, hon."

"Whitney?"

That sister raised her brows. "Dude, I don't even *have* a Mark."

She stood there, stunned. Okay, her Mark was doing a happy little pulsy thing and the tingles *were* traveling on to her pleasurable pink bits, but… Her?

Scarlet turned her attention to Keller and Madden. "Me?"

Keller winked and Madden…smiled? Sort of a mix between a grimace and a smile. A smilace? She saw the vulnerability in his eyes, the wariness and unwillingness to let her in. In one sweeping glance, she caught it all. This was the big, bad pack protector who probably didn't let anyone in. Keller would be the politician. Granted, the man could probably tear off a wolf's head without hesitation, but Madden would be the one knocking heads around first and asking questions never.

At least Garron and Quentin were able to walk away.

"Yes, Miss Wickham, you."

She looked to Madden for confirmation. His nod didn't do anything for the butterflies in her stomach. "Um, okay. I don't know how… Do I… Like, lean forward and you can sniff me or…"

Scarlet waved her hands, gesturing between them. She so wasn't knowledgeable about wolf-land specifics. Sure, she'd absorbed the laws Gabby had spouted, but she hadn't bothered with the rest. Hell, she didn't even know who the Ruling Alphas *were*, hadn't seen a picture or learned their names. She just knew that they were their starting point in Operation: Help Whitney.

Once again, like when she was a child, she should have paid more attention.

"Why don't we meet in the hotel's restaurant for dinner? We can talk and…see how things go from there." Keller's words were soft and soothing while a sexual, predatory gleam lingered in Madden's eyes. She imagined him unleashing his pent-up need. On her.

She shivered, a brush of arousal traveling down her spine. Okay. Yeah. Dinner. She licked her lips. "That sounds good. Seven?"

That'd give them enough time to develop a battle plan. The growing throb in her shoulder told her in more than words that these two were the ones for her. She'd be the balance between the seething strength of Madden and the hidden power of Keller.

And that didn't scare her nearly as much as it should have. Like, at all.

*

Madden watched her walk away, watched the sisters Wickham push and nudge through the throng until they were hidden from sight.

His wolf was *pissed.*

His heart thundered, pounding against his chest like a thousand horses racing across the plains. He couldn't draw air into his lungs, couldn't breathe.

His beast clawed and scraped and scratched inside him, snarling because he and Keller had let Scarlet leave.

17

The woman awed him. Not only did her body call to him, her mind proved she'd be a good match for them. She hadn't walked into the Gathering blind. No, their mate had come in armed, prepared to battle with the overbearing Alphas.

Madden never doubted they were arrogant. Alphas, as a rule, wanted things done now and their way. Period.

Their Scarlet would be a good supporter and adversary at the same time.

"She's beautiful." Keller's voice was pitched low, but Madden had no trouble hearing his partner Alpha.

And he agreed. She had luscious curves in all of the right places, nothing like the trim unmarked female wolves who threw themselves at the Ruling Alpha pair. Female wolves were great for a tumble, but their temperament didn't provide proper balance, hence the magic that forced Alphas to find their mates amongst the human Marked.

And their Marked, with her round hips and lush breasts, was perfect.

Her long brown hair had seemed to gleam and glow in the ballroom, catching the light with her every shift. Her eyes… Her eyes were dark chocolate, the deep hue tempting him and luring him closer.

And, wolf or no, he was a chocolate lover at heart.

Keller's elbow collided with his stomach, and Madden grunted. "What?"

"What do you think?"

He had only one thought, and he and his wolf were in complete agreement. "Mine."

"Ours."

The wolf growled but quickly recognized their partner's claim. The beast knew they couldn't rule, couldn't claim Scarlet, alone. They needed Keller. Keller was as bloodthirsty as he was, but the other wolf managed to keep him out of trouble. His presence prevented Madden from spiriting Scarlet away and locking her up somewhere safe. He could protect her if she stayed inside. In his room. He suddenly realized why princesses were locked in towers.

Madden nodded. "Ours."

The low clearing of a throat forced him to turn his attention from the point where Scarlet disappeared, to the man beside them. "Alphas."

The Captain of the Guard. That's right, they'd booted the asshole duo of Quentin and Garron. He hated both men. Their dominance tended to lean a little closer to mean than he liked, but each Alpha pair was entitled to join the Gathering and to search for their mate among the attending Marked.

Marked. He'd found his, theirs.

"Captain." Madden's attention remained riveted on the guard.

"The Colson Alphas were secured transportation to their home and given an escort to the airport." The guard glanced at his watch. "Their flight leaves in one hour, twenty-seven minutes."

19

"Excellent." Keller joined their conversation, turning away from a pair of Alphas who'd approached them.

Keller's gaze fell to him, eyes dark, brows furrowed and lips pinched in a solid white line. Already his partner had to be feeling the effects of their mate's absence.

*Scarlet?* Keller spoke with his partner Alpha telepathically, a benefit of being part of an Alpha pair.

Madden rolled his eyes. *Like I'd ever forget about ensuring her safety.* "Captain, please locate the sisters Wickham. I want them to have round the clock protection. Pull in whomever you need, but I want a guard on their asses at all times. Like fucking glue." The Captain raised a single brow but remained silent. Madden refused to sate the guard's curiosity. The packs would learn about Scarlet soon enough. "That's all I need."

The wolf bowed and retreated, disappearing into the sea of men and women.

His inner-beast clawed at him, furious he'd let Scarlet's protection fall to another.

A rough nudge had him turning his attention to Keller. "Chill. We're having dinner with her tonight. Probably more. Then we can both watch over her."

Madden knew he'd been at Keller's side since they were young, but it still creeped him out when the man read his mind.

"I know." Knowing didn't keep the wolf calm. He practically vibrated with the need to hunt and protect her. She was so small and sweet and—

20

Keller snorted. "Small, maybe. I don't think our mate exudes sweetness."

Fucker had weaseled into his head again. Madden growled at the other wolf. The beast wouldn't tolerate anyone, not even Keller, speaking badly about Scarlet. "She was protecting hers. She—"

"Alphas."

He turned and snarled at the wolf who'd interrupted them, then drew the sound back. He was on edge, would be until Scarlet carried their bite and they both came deep within her body, one in her ass, the other in her pussy.

There was no reason to snap off Albert's head. "Sorry."

Keller strode past him, hand patting Madden's chest. There wasn't a sexual relationship between them, but time brought easy familiarity and comfort most human men shunned. "Don't mind grumpy here. What do you need?"

Madden needed Scarlet, but it didn't look like he'd get his way any time soon.

"The Marked have all checked in, though we still have a few Alpha pairs yet to arrive. I have confirmed they'll be here by morning."

"Thank you, Albert." Keller gave the man a small nod and the wolf scampered away.

Keller, eyes dancing with mirth, turned to Madden. "That wasn't very nice."

"Shut it. You know you feel the same way; you're simply nicer about it. You want to hunt her, too." He narrowed his eyes. "Maybe we should have picked her guards ourselves. I'll go find the Captain—"

His partner chuckled. "Come on, we still have a few duties to complete before we can meet our mate, and I'm sure the Captain has selected the very best to watch over the sisters Wickham."

The wolf growled but felt the truth in Keller's words.

He just didn't like it.

# CHAPTER THREE

The closer she drew to the restaurant, the hotter her Mark became. It sent pulses of arousal thrumming through her veins. With every step her pleasure grew, body heating, and her doubts about Keller and Madden melted away. The first response was the gentle tingles, the hum to signify her mates' closeness. Then she'd become aroused, burning with need until they completed their bond. It increased until she was desperate for their bodies.

The only good thing about the process was that the wolves would feel the same. Their need would mirror hers, and a burning sensation would pierce them in the identical place as where she carried her Mark.

They'd all be a bubble of arousal until they finally broke.

Yum.

The only thing marring her impending mating was the fact that she still hadn't hunted up the Ruling Alphas to sort out Whitney's situation. Plus, there was some guy with a gun on his hip following her.

She seriously hoped she wasn't about to be involved in another incident like the one in the ballroom. One confrontation a day was enough for her. Really.

Scarlet tugged on the hem of her skirt, nudging down the edge. She never should have listened to Gabby. The darned thing rose with every step. She wobbled a little on her high heels, the four-inch, strappy stilettos making it difficult to walk. Ugh.

Plus, what had been up with her sister? Gabriella had been giving her extra-wide smiles and battering her with taunting questions.

"Isn't it great that your mates are *so* strong?"

"I bet they're as strong as the Ruling Alphas."

"I wonder if…"

And blah, blah, blah. The woman knew something Scarlet didn't, and as soon as she was done with the whole mating thing, she'd beat it out of her sister.

Scarlet continued clicking down the wide, marble-tiled hallway, passing boutique after boutique of overpriced souvenirs and gifts. Nearing a store boasting high-end purses and accessories, she paused, pretending to look over the offerings. In reality, she took a peek at Mr. Gun Guy in the glass' reflection.

He didn't even pretend he wasn't watching her. No, he stood eight feet back, hands behind him, and flat-out stared at her.

Well, she wasn't about to have him follow her to dinner. She turned and faced him head on. "Is there a reason you're following me?"

"Yes." His voice was a low baritone, but it did nothing for her.

She waited for further explanation but didn't get anything. "Okay, why?"

The man's look remained bland. "Because the Ruling Alphas ordered your protection."

She rolled her eyes. "Well, we're back to why."

"It was ordered."

Scarlet huffed. "Do you know why and you're not telling me, or are you simply a drone doing as he's told?"

That earned her a quick twitch of his lips, and she knew he was trying to suppress a smile. "A little in between."

"Fine. God forbid we complain about the Ruling Alphas and their high handedness. This is because my sisters and I got into it in the ballroom with Garron and Quentin, isn't it? Keller and Madden tattled to them. It wasn't our fault, you know." Then again, the assholes had been tossed from the Gathering, so it made sense that the head honchos needed to be informed. "Well, if you're gonna follow me around like a puppy," she winked to take some of the sting out of her insult, "you might as well walk next to me."

Scarlet gestured for the guard to approach, but the man stood still, his body frozen in indecision.

"Come on, I promise not to tell the big bad Ruling Alphas you actually *talked* to me while you acted as my guard. Hell, who knows when I'll actually get to meet them. I'll probably forget you by then." She winced. "Not that you're forgettable, I—" She huffed. "Just talk to me."

"I don't think—"

"Well, I do."

She stomped toward him and tugged on his arm, ignoring the sting that accompanied touching a male not meant for her. Stupid Mark. Now that she'd met her mates, pain would accompany any contact she had with other men, human or wolf. At least until she completed her mating with Keller and Madden. Thankfully she wasn't alone in the ouchy department. It was the same way for the guys.

"Yes, Alpha Mate." The man grumbled but relented. Aw, her males had already spread the word about their connection. That had to be the reason she'd been upgraded from simply "Marked" to "Alpha Mate" by the guard. How sweet. Sweetish. She sorta wished they hadn't jumped the gun, but Alphas were Alphas.

As uncomfortable as the wolf appeared, she didn't bother trying to talk to him further. She simply felt better that he wasn't following her and making her feel like a stalked chubby gazelle.

In less than a minute, they strode into the restaurant side by side, the maître d' quickly leading them toward the back. Together, they wove their way through the room, sliding around various tables, and she noticed most were occupied by two men and a single woman.

Well, it looked like quite a few were already performing the Test of Proximity. Although she had a feeling the test was all for show. Much like the dinner she was about to enjoy.

Before long, she stood before her two wolves in the very back of the restaurant, and both men rose upon her approach. It was Madden's growl that broke the sweet moment.

She needed to remember he was the more aggressive of the two, and apparently he didn't like other men close to her.

Hoping her mother's teachings had been correct, she stepped in front of the guard, redirecting the wolf's attention. "Madden?"

The rolling sound cut off the moment his eyes met hers, the last of his air hissing from his lungs in a sigh. "Scarlet."

She waved behind her. "The Ruling Alphas said I needed a guard. No need to get testy."

Madden furrowed his brow. "Wha—"

Keller cut him off. "I'm sure they want to keep you safe." He smiled and stepped around the table, drawing her forward with a hand on her lower back. The seductive scents of heated wood, raw power and man surrounded her, and she melted into his side. "You already know how to handle our Madden."

She chanced a look at the wolf in question and noted his smile. "Perhaps." She turned her attention back to Keller. "I'm not sure how to handle you, though."

"I doubt that'll be a problem, sweet. I'm like any other wolf. Give me something to snack on and you'll have my attention." She didn't miss Keller's not-so-subtle innuendo.

"Right," she drawled.

Keller pulled out the chair and she sat between the two men. His heat warred with the inferno that flowed from Madden. Two sides of the same coin, so alike, yet so different.

The guard that had accompanied her took up a post in front of the table. He and four others essentially made a wall-o-wolves, cutting them off from the rest of the diners. Talk about overkill.

*

Keller forced himself not to reveal all. She didn't know. Didn't realize she was to be mated to the Ruling Alphas. And that made him want her all the more.

*Truly?* Madden's voice floated to him, and he sensed his partner's vulnerability mixed with surprise. They'd had their share of women come after them because of their position, but this human Marked had no idea as to their identities.

Truly.

His shoulder throbbed, the heat slithering through him and wrapping around his cock. He couldn't deny the scents of arousal surrounding them: her sweet musk combining with his need and Madden's desire. He'd long ago brushed aside any embarrassment over his partner's reactions when it came to women. From the moment they'd paired, they'd shared women, preparing themselves for their mate someday. Bodies touched, cocks got hard. It was all part of sex. As long as lips didn't wander and swords didn't cross, they were all good.

He fought to stifle his moan when Scarlet's tongue darted out to lick her lips.

It didn't work. A pale blush stole up her cheeks, and she glanced at him. "What? What are you looking at?"

He smiled. He couldn't suppress the sappy grin that covered his features. "You."

Madden eased toward her, closing in on her from the other side, and Keller mirrored him. The flavors of need grew, encompassing their small group. He knew she didn't recognize mates by scent, couldn't smell their desire. Part of him wished his sweet Marked was another wolf and could sense their flavors in the air. But when she turned those brown eyes on him, so needy, he didn't care that she would always wear human skin and never fur.

Keller's shoulder seemed to be on fire, scorching him and stroking his cock with an imaginary hand. He moaned and leaned even closer, catching more of her scent, hissing when the heat grew and his balls drew up tight.

"I don't understand…" Scarlet shook her head as if clearing her mind.

Madden nuzzled her from behind, rubbing his scruff along the pale skin of her neck. Keller watched dark fur slide from his pores, evidence of the man's wolf rising and pushing at his control.

Keller felt the same, beast pouncing and shoving at the wall that held it at bay. But he needed to go slow, needed to keep from stripping his mate and taking her in front of one and all. He was normally the more level-headed of the two. Normally.

"Shh…" He eased back, forcing his muscles to relax, and he shoved at his wolf. "Madden, give her some space." His partner's eyes glowed bright. "Man, you're scaring her. Knowing and feeling are two different things." The other wolf whimpered, and it was the first time he'd ever seen his partner truly vulnerable.

Keller reached out and ran a finger down her cheek, traced her jaw. The heat rose around them. "A kiss for Madden, Scarlet? You can see he lives close to the edge."

Her arousal beat at his control. She was a Marked, knew of Gathering laws, and he assumed she was familiar with what happened when meeting her mates. But like he said, knowing and feeling were two different things.

Scarlet nodded and turned her head, a small movement that put her lips within Madden's reach. His partner struck, mouth moving over hers, and tongue delving into her. Keller's cock throbbed in his pants, silently demanding release, but he held it back. Watching them, their mouths dancing, tongues twining... Envy and jealousy had no place in their mating. All he felt was pure bliss.

Madden's feelings flowed over their connection, the peacefulness that came from experiencing Scarlet's touch. He sensed his partner's desperate need, a feeling greater than his own, and he accepted that encouraging Scarlet to turn to Madden first was the right decision.

They had a lifetime together.

The seconds ticked by, the entwined couple's breathing growing heavier with every heartbeat.

Madden?

Mine.

Keller sighed. They'd go through this until they'd claimed her. They were both dominant, but Madden's wolf had always been a little more so. *Ours, Madden.*

A snarl tore through his mind.

Madden, we need to take care of our mate. I'm sure she's hungry.

This time it was a growl, but their kiss eased, lessening until his partner released their woman.

Scarlet sat back with a sigh, fingers trembling when she reached for her water glass.

"Scarlet?" The last thing he wanted to do was overwhelm her.

Scarlet licked her lips, and a light blush tinged her cheeks. "Sorry. It was so…"

"Big." He tempted himself with the feel of her skin beneath his hand. He stroked her arm, letting his fingers slide over her softness. He wanted her no less than Madden, but he didn't want to scare his poor Marked.

"Yeah," her whisper reached his sensitive ears and then she turned toward him, glowing smile in place. "Big."

He echoed her expression, let her feelings clasp him. "But big is good."

Scarlet nodded, closed the distance between them. "Big can be very, very good."

She brushed her mouth across his, her delicate tongue darting out to lap at his lips, and he resisted the urge to surge into her. He couldn't, wouldn't, overpower her with the depth of his need. Madden lacked control, but Keller's passion had always outpaced his partner's.

The arousal that had been simmering nearly bubbled over, the feelings so much stronger than what he'd caught from Madden. Reluctantly, he ended their near-chaste kiss, eased from her mouth and put distance between them. They were both panting, fighting to catch their breath.

"Dinner. We invited you out for dinner." He swallowed, mouth dry.

"I vote for dessert." Madden's voice was deep and hoarse. A glance revealed the wolf was almost in control.

Scarlet turned back to Madden. While he couldn't see her expression, he could see his partner's. She reached out and cupped the other wolf's cheek. He saw the sappy smile that graced his features. Keller was awed when the smattering of fur receded to reveal skin. He didn't listen to her low words; he merely enjoyed seeing the tension recede from Madden.

Yes, she was the perfect one for them.

# CHAPTER FOUR

"Easy big guy." She rubbed her thumb along Madden's pronounced cheekbone. "We'll get there. Soon."

Scarlet's heart thundered, pummeling her rib cage as fear and need warred. Part of her ached to listen to Madden: to do as her body asked and follow them up to their room to solidify their bond.

Her Mark throbbed in an ever-increasing rhythm, each pulse reaching down to stroke her clit. Her nipples were hard within her top, pressing and straining against her silk and lace bra.

Their arousal was palpable. Even without their sensitive noses, she sensed their desire. For her. *Her*. Curvy, plump Scarlet Wickham. A nobody.

Keller and Madden's nearness wreaked havoc on her body. She wanted to rub against them and purr like a cat. Yet she also ached to run and hide from the feelings their closeness elicited.

She had no delusions of a forever love or immediate appearance of deep emotions, but…but the Mark laid down the building blocks. It fed their emotions and encouraged them to bloom.

And there was some kind of blooming.

Her heart was already engaged with these two massive Alphas. While Madden seemed intense, Keller was banked aggression. The larger wolf charged in, and her other mate was more watchful but no less fierce.

"I still vote for dessert." Madden's voice no longer held the rough scratch of his wolf, but she saw it lurking beneath his skin.

Damn, she wanted them both. Ached for them to release their passions and claim her. Every part of her being screamed for their touch. There was only one thing she could do.

She'd calmed the raging wolf, and now she was about to poke him with a stick. Yum.

Turning from Madden, she gave Keller her attention. She noted the hint of yellow in his eyes, the sprinkle of barely-there fur along his cheeks and the flash of fang when he smiled. Her sweeter mate was on the edge.

"Keller?" She couldn't breathe, lungs frozen from the choice she was about to voice.

"Yes, sweet?" He eased closer, his heavy scent enveloping her.

"I think it's time for dessert."

The man's eyes did flicker yellow, then gray fur sprouted and coated his skin. A snarl echoed behind her, but her attention was focused on the battle warring across Keller's features. The wolf wanted out, she saw it, but the human half of him wouldn't let it free. He kept it caged and locked up tight.

She couldn't have that.

Claw tipped fingers gripped her upper arms, and she was yanked back, Madden's form molding against her.

"Mine." His snarl overrode every other sound in the room.

Sharp fangs scraped along her exposed neck, and a shudder overtook her body causing arousal to slam into her. She tilted her head to the side, encouraging Madden's attentions, letting the fierce wolf sample her.

Through it all, she kept her gaze on Keller, daring and taunting him with her intent focus.

Reaching up, she threaded her fingers through Madden's hair, ran her digits through his strands. He licked and sucked her skin, stoking her desire with each touch.

When his tongue traced her ear, she moaned and gasped, pussy flooding with moisture. She wanted him, them. Now.

Scarlet squeezed her thighs together, taking pleasure in the pressure and working to alleviate some of the blissful ache surrounding her clit. Her heat clenched, tightening, and even more cream soaked her panties.

Before her, Keller's nostrils flared, his wolf catching her scent.

Madden's growls and groans intruded, adding to her panting moans. "Need."

The word was barely recognizable, but she sympathized. Need was one way to put it. Soul deep craving was another, but whatever.

His large, warm hand stroked her side, squeezing gently before continuing its travels. The touch shifted and rose along her rib cage to cup her left breast.

His callused palm easily engulfed her plump mound. He squeezed and kneaded her flesh, thumb circling her hard nipple. The added touch sent another zing of ecstasy rocketing through her, heading to her needy pussy.

"Madden," she gasped and moaned, pressing into his touch.

And still Keller observed them, eyes entirely yellow and glowing in the dim restaurant. His muscles were tense, straining beneath his skin.

She wanted him to lose control, let all that tension free.

Madden sucked on her neck, adding in a piercing nibble between licks.

"God, yes. Mate." She moaned and rocked in her chair, searching for added pressure against her pussy.

Then her wishes were answered. Madden abandoned her breast, his hand wandering down her stomach, over the slight swell, and his fingers fisted her skirt. The hem rose higher and higher, increasing her arousal with each climbing inch. Cool air bathed her soaked, silk covered pussy.

She suddenly remembered their guards, but a quick glance revealed they still stood before the table, backs to them, and blocking their view of the restaurant. Okay, maybe guards came in handy. She'd have to thank the Ruling Alphas.

But now, she thanked God for her mates.

Thanked God because Madden's fingers traced her inner-thigh, his digits drawing nearer and nearer to her heated pussy. She reached behind her, mimicked his movements and gripped his upper leg.

When his palm cupped her cunt, she grabbed his cock. When he traced her panty-clad slit, she stroked his dick.

Their actions mirrored. Rubbing, petting, pumping, and then the silk of her knickers disappeared.

All the while she watched Keller. Still, silent Keller.

"Do you see, Keller?" She panted and fought for breath.

Madden growled and groaned, yanking the same sounds from her chest when he delved between her folds. Blunt fingertips slid through her cream, rubbing her from hole to clit and back again.

Then…oh, fuck…then he pushed into her, shoving his fingers into her cunt and stretching her with his invasion.

"Mine." The snarl was rough against her neck. His digits withdrew and pushed back in, tearing a choked cry from her throat. "Mine."

Scarlet continued tormenting Madden's cock as he plunged his fingers in and out of her wet hole.

"Do you see him fucking me?" The heel of the larger wolf's hand pressed hard against her clit, sending a shard of pleasure through her. "God, Keller, he's fucking me, gonna make me come."

37

Madden shifted her, his right arm coming around her body and he squeezed her breast. "Ride me mate, come for me." Scarlet rocked her hips in time with his thrusts, fighting to do as her mate demanded. "She's so wet and tight, Keller. Gonna suck our dicks right in. Squeeze so hard."

She arched into his touch, drawing on the pleasure of his fingers and hands. He pinched her nipple and thrust into her pussy, gripped her breast and stroked her G-spot. It all joined and coalesced, building within her as it grew and grew.

"He's fucking me, Keller. Do you know how wet I am? I can't wait for you both to fuck me, claim me." Madden slammed in and out of her heat with bruising speed. "Is this how you'll fuck me?"

She panted and moaned, fighting for her release, gobbling up every morsel of pleasure Madden handed over.

The wet sounds of the wolf's thrust and retreat surrounded them, her scorching musk adding to the air. She knew the other wolves could hear and smell what they were doing, but she only had eyes for her self-restrained mate.

Scarlet was so close to coming, racing toward the edge of release. The pleasure built, growing and expanding to fill her from top to bottom. It crept into her toes, taking over her muscles, and she arched. Control was no longer hers, stolen by Madden's ministrations until all she could do was feel.

"Need... Wanna..." She sobbed, stared at Keller and saw when the moment of indecision shattered.

Keller leaned forward and fisted her hair. His fingers slid through the strands and jerked her head toward him. He snarled, baring his fangs. She'd broken his hardened shell. "Come."

He pressed their mouths together, shoving his tongue deep into her. They tangled, yet he dominated their coming together. He forced her to his will and she eagerly followed, reveling in her triumph.

The bliss that had been gathering blew, bursting into a million sparkling fireworks. The bright lights glowed behind her eyelids. She came with a blinding rush, muscles spasming, tensing and tightening until her chest stilled.

She couldn't breathe, couldn't think beyond the two men bracketing her. She was surrounded, encased in her mates. She trembled within Madden's embrace, let Keller draw her into him, and her orgasm kept racing through her veins.

The infinite bliss racked her, tore her apart from inside out, and she sobbed against her mate's mouth.

Distantly she heard growls and snarls, the sounds breaking through her pleasure-induced haze. Suddenly her men were gone. They'd built an impenetrable wall between her and whoever had invaded their space, their bliss.

She hoped they ripped the intruders into a billion pieces.

Unsteadily, she pushed to standing, catching herself on the chair as she rose. On wobbly feet, she peeked around the bodies. Garron and Quentin were being held back by a guard, the row of strips on his sleeve indicating that he was the Captain.

Her mates met the danger with rolling growls, but the other two wolves didn't appear threatened.

No, Garron opened his mouth and yelled into the tense space. "We call right of challenge! We challenge the Ruling Alphas!"

Scarlet gasped. No. Not only were her mates being challenged, but... Her mates were the Ruling Alphas? No. No, no, no. She was not the right girl for the job. Ever. Never ever, even.

But it was too late. A low exclamation of "witnessed" came from the other side of the restaurant. The word dashed her hopes that her mates, her Ruling Alphas, could get out of the situation without a fight.

Keller sighed, and she knew what he'd say before the word left his mouth. Part of her wanted to silence him, slap her hand over his lips so he couldn't say a word. But the challenge had been witnessed, and it had to go on.

"Accepted."

# Chapter Five

"Only you," Gabby grumped. "Only you would come to our first Gathering and, without realizing it, snag the Ruling Alphas."

"You knew? Why didn't you tell me so I didn't make an ass of myself?" Scarlet glared at her sister.

"Because it was fun." Gabby stuck out her tongue. "And, amazingly enough, if you'd listened to me at any point before this moment, you would have known about them, too. Funny how that works." Gabby glared back at her, and Scarlet realized that her sister was right. Damn it. "Anyway. *Then*, you'd be the only one whose Alphas were challenged for rank *and* mate." Gabs huffed. "Have they decided to let you keep the cat or is he going to be a snack?"

She wanted to laugh. Almost. Burger would shred them before becoming dinner. He was a fierce little feline.

But her belly churned, nerves rolling and rumbling in her stomach as she watched the clock tick toward eight. Her mates had retreated to their rooms to prepare, requiring solitude while they got ready for the fight to come. A fight to the death.

She'd been sad to see them go, stride off to seclusion, but had understood. Since their mating was incomplete, the guys wouldn't be able to focus on the coming fight with her hanging around. They'd be too concerned with how they could finagle her into bed. And, being the Ruling Alphas, strongest of the wolves across the nation, their need to mate was more pressing than most.

But suddenly, Gabby's words interrupted Scarlet's thoughts.

Scarlet froze for a moment and focused on her sister. "Wait. Challenge for mate? Can they do that?"

Gabby rolled her eyes. "Duh. Have you been listening?"

"Don't 'duh' me, woman," she snapped. Damn it, Scarlet should have paid better attention to all those rules thrown at her during the flight.

Gabby rolled her eyes. Again. "If the challengers are unmated, they can fight for simply rank, or rank and mate if they feel the female belongs to them. Garron and Quentin claim that you're actually theirs, and you're only after Keller and Madden because of their position."

Rage, pure, hot, molten rage overtook Scarlet. "Those assholes."

"We could kill them. That would be fun." Whitney bounced over, faux smile in place, the expression not quite meeting her eyes.

"Bloodthirsty, much?" Scarlet looked her sister over, noting the fatigue that lined her face. She reached out and snagged her sister's hand, tugging her close. "What's up with you, babe?"

Whitney leaned her head against her shoulder and snuggled close. This was how it'd always been between them. Scarlet was their leader, their protector. Gabby got to be the loud mouthed, obnoxiously adorable brat, and the two of them protected emotional Whitney.

"I went back to the registration table to talk to them about my lack of Mark, and they told me to come back in the morning. The Wardens should arrive tomorrow and they're who I need to talk to about this stuff. So, for now, I'm stuck in butt sniffing limbo."

Scarlet squeezed her waist in a small hug. "Well, I've got an 'in' with the Ruling Alphas so the Warden guys won't have a choice about helping you. We'll figure it out. And, hey, at least the sniffers are hot, right? I mean, if they're gonna get up close and personal, we should be happy they're attractive."

A low growl warned her that her mates had come upon them, but it was Keller who spoke. "Who's attractive?"

The growl deepened.

Sighing, she turned around to face Madden and Keller. Without hesitation, she snapped her fingers in Madden's direction, frown firmly in place. "Enough. You know I'm yours. I know I'm yours. The three of us are a big ball of yours."

Keller's laugh followed her words, and happiness danced in his eyes. The man didn't laugh nearly enough. It sounded hoarse and rarely used.

Whitney's giggle joined Keller, and Gabby's snicker followed them. Poor Madden frowned, deep furrows between his eyes, and she strode toward him. Before he protested or pulled away, she wiped away the lines.

"Calm down. You need to save your grump for Garron and Quentin." That got her a snarl, and she rolled her eyes. Without having to look, she reached out and tugged Keller close so she could wrap an arm around his waist.

"I expect you to both kick ass." She shoved the idea that they'd fail aside, blinked away the threatening tears, and tipped her head back. She flashed him a forced, cheerful grin. "And fast, please. I'd rather not to have to wait for you two to heal before we get down and dirty."

Keller's expression turned wicked, and the rough texture of Madden's five o'clock shadow scraped against her neck. A shiver of arousal snaked through her, and her mates breathed deep. She had no doubt they could scent the musk of her juices.

Ah, the joy of being mated to wolves.

The man she now recognized as the Captain of the Ruling Alphas' guard cleared his throat and stepped into her line of sight. "Alphas, it's time."

Scarlet's heart stuttered. The next few minutes would determine their fate. She had faith in her men; they hadn't achieved their position through a democracy. They'd fought tooth and claw to rise above the rest. But that didn't mean they couldn't be injured.

She grabbed Madden's hand and squeezed, snaring his attention. "I know you want to gut them. I know." His growl confirmed her statement. "But you need to fight smart, not strong. They're bullies. Neither of them have any control. If they did, they wouldn't have approached us like they did. You get them angry and let them make a mistake. Just don't

44

let them do that to *you*, you hear me?" She squeezed again. "I need you back, safe and whole, Madden."

The large wolf took a deep breath and a look of calm swept across him as he exhaled. "Yes, mate."

She turned to Keller, her less outwardly aggressive mate. "I know you don't want to kill them, but this is to the death, Keller. They won't settle for anything less, and you need to go into this knowing that four walk in and only two walk out. They want your position. They want me."

He snarled, baring his elongated teeth. "Never."

Scarlet jerked her head in a quick nod. "Good. I'd kiss you, but I need you hungry for them, not me."

That got her the reaction she'd expected, both men chuckling as they turned to follow the Captain toward the center of the ballroom. The packs had to be paying a pretty penny to allow the desecration of carpet, but Scarlet wasn't about to ask questions. Hell, for all she knew, the hotel was pack owned.

"Alphas." The Captain bowed and brushed past them, on toward the center of the circle the watchers had formed. A wide space was left empty, bodies lining the area.

"We've gathered to witness a challenge between the Ruling Alphas and the Colson Alphas." A murmur went through the crowd. "Alphas, step forward."

Madden turned her toward him, hands gripping her shoulders, and he kissed her. He plunged his tongue into her mouth, sweeping into her in a grand stroke and she submitted to his assault. As quickly as it began, it ended, her mate placing her apart from him.

"Win for me." She was panting, breathless.

"Always." He strode toward the waiting Captain.

Then it was Keller's turn, her mate drawing her forward and giving her a gentle kiss. He gifted her with a soft caress of his tongue against hers that left her equally panting when he pulled away.

"They're going to underestimate you. They're not going to be prepared for the ass-whipping you're about to lay down. But you're an Alpha, Keller. Show them."

He nodded, brushed one last chaste kiss over her lips and then he was following Madden to the center of the ring.

Whitney wrapped an arm around her waist, resting her head on her shoulder. "They'll be fine."

Gabby twined her fingers with Scarlet's. "They haven't fought their way to the top for nothing. They'll kick ass, and then they'll boink you all night. It's all good."

Silence descended, both pairs of Alphas standing before the Captain. "This is a challenge to the death for position and mate. Each Alpha pair shall fight. One on two legs, the other on four." A soft murmur went through the crowd, but the Captain ignored the sounds. "Alphas, please prepare. The challenge shall begin once the first wolf has completed his shift."

With that, he stepped back, and the scariest moments of Scarlet's life began.

46

Keller didn't hesitate. He tore at his shirt, and ripped his slacks, cloth parting beneath his shifting claws. Fur pushed through his pores in a gentle wave. His bones reshaped and muscles shortened, body taking on the form of his beast. No pain assaulted him. No, it was pure pleasure at the wolf being released to defend their position, their mate.

He kept his gaze on the other shifting wolf, noting with satisfaction that it was the larger of the two mirroring him. Scarlet had been correct: the Colson Alphas were sloppy and quick to anger, and Keller would use that to his benefit. The other wolf might be larger and stronger, but Keller was faster. He'd dart in and out, scratch and claw the other beast until it lost control. Then he'd win.

Madden stood tense at his side, hands fisted and knuckles white with restrained rage. Keller felt the anger, the controlled fury bubbling beneath the skin and pumping through veins.

He prided himself on the swiftness of his change, and in less than five seconds he was on four feet. The other wolf, Garron, was still engaged in his shift, legs reshaping to his beast's form. Tanned skin had given way to gray fur, and the man outweighed him by at least fifty pounds.

*Now.* Keller roared to his partner as he leapt across the space separating them.

Madden's bellow echoed through his mind and rang through the room. From his periphery, he watched the massive man keep pace with him.

A beefy fist collided with Quentin, and that was the last sight of his two-legged partner that reached him. His world became narrowed to a view of fur and flesh.

Garron attacked quickly, a flash of fangs that snapped at him upon his approach. Keller was faster, ducking and retaliating with a bite of his own. His teeth tightened on the wolf's foreleg and blood flowed over his tongue.

Keller the man was disgusted by the raw taste. Keller the wolf gloried in the strike and savored the other man's honeyed, copper fluid.

First blood.

Except Garron reacted in kind, sinking his wicked teeth into his back and biting into his flesh, the wound much too close to Keller's spine for comfort.

He released the other wolf, and it danced back only to dart forward once again. Keller jumped aside, digging his teeth into his opponent's hindquarter as he passed. More blood. More of that goodness. His wolf salivated, aching to taste the interloper once again.

But Garron's attack hadn't failed completely. A throbbing pain erupted along his side, the ache pulsing with every beat of his heart. Wetness coated his ribs, and he knew his enemy had injured him.

But he couldn't dwell on the wound. Not when Garron spun on him, rising to his hind legs. He countered, balancing and meeting the attack. The Colson Alpha snapped his teeth, fighting to bite Keller's vulnerable throat, but only managing to gouge his muzzle.

Garron's nails dug into his shoulders, sinking past fur and skin deep into him. More of his blood crept forth. Keller pushed back the blossoming hurt.

The enemy wouldn't win, no matter how hard he tried.

Keller remained upright and dug his claws into the other wolf's fur, searching for skin and flesh that lurked out of sight.

His competitor broke off from their clench, stumbling, but he didn't let the wolf wander far. Keller pounced, mouth opening wide and then it was filled with the wolf's protective fur. He fought to breathe, drawing in air past the blood that filled his nostrils. Fuck. Had the bastard broken his nose?

Increasing the pressure of his bite, he was rewarded with a rush Garron's of blood filling his mouth. Applying further force gave him the crack of bone.

Garron pulled and yanked against his hold, snarling barks interspersed with whimpers. Keller had managed to slow the larger wolf, his attack breaking a leg.

He released and danced back, moving out of reach and he watched the other wolf limp back and forth. Garron's gaze absorbed everything, and Keller did the same. His enemy's hobble was easily noticeable. Blood flowed freely from the wound, and a bone poked through the skin. The other wolf's muzzle bled sluggishly, but the hindquarter released more and more viscous fluid with each beat of his heart.

The enemy wolf was close to the end. Its chest heaved with every breath, expanding and contracting in an ever-increasing rhythm.

He distantly heard grunts and groans from Madden's fight, the collision of flesh against flesh coming with regularity. But few of the sounds came from his partner.

Keller flashed his fangs, curling his upper lip until the gleaming lengths were visible.

A bellow of rage reached him, and he stretched his mind to Madden. *Easy. Don't fall into his trap, Madden.*

He didn't have time to say much more. Not when Garron rushed forward and pounced on him, shoving him until he lay beneath the larger wolf.

A shout reached him, the single word from Scarlet's mouth working to bolster his strength. "No!"

Keller worked his back legs, clawing the vulnerable underbelly of his attacker while he used his forelegs to keep the man's life-ending teeth from his neck. A mixture of his and Garron's blood surrounded him. His enemy didn't simply snapped at him with deadly teeth. No, claws scraped and shredded him as he lay supine on the ground.

Enough.

He gathered his strength, dug into the part of him he often suppressed, and let his true beast free. He shed the mantle of calm knowledge and peace to reveal a monster.

With a great heave, he shoved Garron from his prone body, rolling them until he stood over the larger wolf.

Part of him, the portion that always worked toward a diplomatic end to any conflict, detested what he was about to do. His other half reveled in the bloodshed. It rejoiced in securing their place at Scarlet's side. They couldn't care less about ruling the North American packs. But nothing would keep them from their mate. Nothing.

That single thought in mind, he lowered his head, opened his mouth wide and then tightened his jaws. He relished the resounding snap of bone as he killed the wolf beneath him.

Fresh, tasty blood flowed freely, and he only allowed the wolf to swallow one mouthful. It fought against his control, aching to finish its meal, but he wrestled the beast into submission. The encounter wasn't about the hunt, but the kill. They'd search out dinner. Later. After they'd secured Scarlet as theirs.

He released the dead wolf and moved away from the body until he was able to sit and catch his breath. Wounds made themselves known, other cuts and bites he'd not noticed, now throbbed in time with his heart. They'd heal soon enough. For now, his attention remained riveted on Quentin and Madden.

Both men were covered in their fair share of blood, the battle made more difficult when fighting without the benefit of sharp teeth and claws.

Madden struck again and again, fists colliding with Quentin's cheek, chin then stomach. It was a constantly shifting dance of pain, the two men hunting for the opportunity to end the fight. Permanently.

Quentin noticed his dead partner and darted away from Madden, heading straight for Keller. The man's eyes had changed to a glowing yellow, showing the wolf was in charge of the human body.

"Nooo…" Quentin's scream was barely recognizable.

The enemy wolf ran toward him, gaze on the dead body at his side. Keller danced away from the corpse, moving with growing stiffness, not wanting to be caught up in the man's madness. It happened sometimes, one partner going insane when they lost half of their pair.

Only…only he'd thought the man was heading for the dead wolf, fighting to get to his deceased partner.

He was wrong.

Quentin shifted with each step, face reforming, fur bursting through skin and hands transforming into claws. Shifting broke the rules and technically ended the fight, but he doubted that'd mean much to the approaching madman.

Keller backed away, working to put distance between him and the looming man. Five feet… Then three… Then…

Madden caught the shifting Alpha mid-pounce, snatched the back of his shirt and yanked the wolf against his chest. In a lightning-fast move, his arms encircled Quentin's neck.

Crack.

Another death complete.

Keller stared at his partner, his brother Alpha, and would have smiled in triumph if he hadn't been in so much pain. Silence surrounded them, and he heard nothing more than their breathing. Adrenaline slipped away, sliding from his blood and leaving him simply a battered, yet victorious, wolf.

# CHAPTER SIX

Scarlet sensed her mates' need vibrating through her, strumming her body like the cords of a guitar, and she was drawn to answer their call.

Unfortunately, due to the dead assholes, she wasn't able to give in. Not when her mates had to clean up and heal from their wounds.

Walking between them through the expansive hallways of the hotel, she kept to their sedate pace. Madden's face was peppered with bruises, and one eye was swollen shut. His lower lip was puffed to twice its normal size with a split on the left side. He didn't make a sound as they traveled, but he did clutch his ribs, a single arm wrapped tight around his chest.

Keller wasn't faring much better. The wound near his hip still bled, albeit much slower than before, and the tear in his side worried her. His fur was matted, blood soaking his gray body. He favored his fore-leg, and the wolf half-hopped alongside her. His muzzle boasted scratches and scrapes, including a bone-deep furrow she imagined had been caused by Garron's fang. More than anything, Scarlet was worried about his blood loss.

Bastard. She wanted to resurrect the dead wolf so she could kick his ass. True, they'd have to hold him down so she could get him good, but she wasn't against breaking the rules.

Two guards led the way, the Captain being one of them, while three followed, including her personal gun-slinger and the Lieutenant. From what she could tell, they were being protected by the best of the Ruling Alpha's soldiers.

Gah. Ruling Alphas. She still hadn't quite gotten over their position. She was a freaking administrative assistant and totally not "ruling anything" material. She'd been expecting a minor set of wolves. Guys that led a pack in Podunk and didn't need a badass woman at their side.

Scarlet took a deep breath. That didn't matter. Fate, or whatever, decided she was supposed to mate the men at her sides, and she would do just that.

Their entourage paused at the elevators, all of them stilling as they waited for the car to arrive. They didn't have to wait long, and the low ding announced its arrival. Fitting into the metal box took a bit of finagling, but eventually the eight of them packed into the small space. This time, the five wolves encircled them while Scarlet, Keller, and Madden had the wall at their backs. Her men repositioned themselves with ease, telling her without words that this was a regular occurrence.

Great. Something fun to look forward to for the rest of her life.

They arrived at the top floor and one of the guards used a special key and card to gain entrance.

Lord, there she found even more guards.

"Seriously?" She'd whispered the words, but every wolf turned their attention to her. Damn furry hearing.

Madden chuckled and then let out a pained groan. It pulled her focus from the surrounding men and back to her mates.

"Okay, Misters, let's get you to bed." Madden's gaze paled to a light yellow, and she rolled her eyes. "To get clean and *heal*. I need some alcohol and gauze and—"

"Alpha Mate?" The low voice of her personal guard reached her. "They'll be fully healed in twelve hours or so. There's no need to worry."

Scarlet spun on him and growled, curling her lip. Damn, her mates had rubbed off on her, making her act more wolfy than human. "And I want them clean and treated. Healing or not, I need to give them what comfort I can." She snapped her fingers. "Hop to it."

That got the men moving. One guard led them to a large bedroom, a massive king-sized bed occupying the center. To the left, she spotted the open door of a bathroom and guided her men in that direction.

She wondered why two Alphas, presumably straight, would share a bedroom and bed, but...

Keller's whimper drew her attention, his wolf pausing half way between the room's entrance and the bathroom.

Brow furrowed, she looked between their destination and her hesitant mate.

"He doesn't want to shower as a wolf and he doesn't have the energy to shift yet. Nobody likes the scent of wet dog." Madden's words were peppered with low, wheezing gasps.

Keller exposed a fang, a deep growl coming from his chest.

55

Scarlet growled back. "You're getting your furry little ass in that bathroom and that's all there is to it." A barely audible, strangled sound came from the doorway, but she ignored it. "I am not getting anywhere near a bed until you two are clean and comfortable. Period." Keller opened his eyes wide, giving her the sweetest puppy dog look. So much for objecting to being considered a dog. "Don't give me that. No naked fun without being clean. I don't know when you'll be well enough to shift, but wouldn't you rather already be blood-free when it happens? We can nap and then you guys may be ready for claiming." She crossed her arms and frowned, watching her four-legged mate.

Strong arms wrapped around her waist, and Madden's heat blanketed her. "Do you want to risk missing out? I'll be making our little mate scream as she comes on my tongue and you'll be stuck showering." He traced her ear, and she shivered. She was a total wolf-whore. For them only, but whore-esque none the less.

Keller growled, but limped past them, moving with determined strides.

Scarlet one, furballs zero.

She figured she wouldn't get to win often with two dominant wolves in the house, so she'd take pleasure in the small victory.

\* \* \*

A soft knock woke her. Or rather, a soft knock followed by surround sound rumbling growls. She smacked their chests in turn, careful of their injuries, and the noise ceased.

"Stop it." She rolled her eyes. "If they wanted to hurt us, do you think they would have knocked?"

The men turned to her, both sets of eyes glowing in the sparse light.

"Don't want anyone to see you." Keller's words were a garbled mess, but she managed to decipher them. Apparently her mate was easygoing when it came to anything but her. At least he was human once again. She had to be thankful for that fact.

"And that's why they tapped on the door. It'll give us a chance to get decent before we let them in. Besides, I'm in your clothes. What are they gonna see?" They'd wanted her naked, but she'd negotiated and ended up in a pair of Keller's boxers and Madden's t-shirt.

If they couldn't feel her skin, she had to wear their scent, and that was final.

If she had to wear their clothes, then they were taking a two hour nap to heal, and *that* was final.

Sighing, she scooted to the end of the bed and frowned at them when their growls grew in volume.

"Stop it." Hey, they listened. Well, that'd come in handy. "You feel like swinging free in front of your guards?"

Scarlet opened the door to allow a wolf to push a table laden with covered dishes into the room. He kept his gaze averted, and she noted a faint tremble going through his body.

She also realized Madden was back to being growly. "For the love of God, Madden, quit it." The guard gasped, but she kept on going. "He's feeding me. You should say 'thank you.' And if that's too hard, the least you could do is not growl at the poor wolf."

Thank goodness for her lessons from her mother. If she let the wolves get away with anything from the get go, they'd act like that for the rest of their lives. There was no way she could deal with snarly men every day.

"Don't like him close to you." She heard the grumble.

"Then you should have gotten dressed and beat me to the door." She gave the wolf a wide smile. "Thank you for bringing dinner. I'm sure they appreciate it even though they're cranky when they just wake up."

The guard's Adam's apple traveled down his throat in a slow procession and, even without a wolf's extra senses, she could tell he was nervous. "You're welcome, Alpha Mate." He bowed. Well, half-bowed since Keller decided to growl then.

The guard spun then practically ran to the door and out of the room. Scarlet turned toward her mates, the men still wrapped in blankets. "What's your problem?"

"We don't like anyone close to you."

"Then you should have gotten out of bed. Didn't we just have this conversation? I know we just had this conversation."

Madden shrugged. "We're trying not to overwhelm you."

She tightened her lips and turned to Keller. "Your idea?" The wolf blushed. "I want you guys as you are. You don't get to modify each other's reactions. That's my job. Even then, I won't be trying to change you, just keep you from killing anyone. With me, you can be yourselves." She propped her hands on her hips. "Did you guys not get the Marked Handbook?"

That earned her two wolfish smiles.

"Being ourselves means dragging you to bed and making you ours." Keller's smile was wicked and matched Madden's.

Scarlet took a step back, shaking her head. "Nope, no nooky until you've eaten and we can check your wounds. Plus, talking would be a good idea. Fun even. Like, gee Scarlet, how has this mating disrupted your world?" She answered herself. "Well, I have to give up my job as an administrative assistant as well as my life in Tampa, that's all. Maybe my cat. Will you eat my cat? Burger is really sweet when he's not peeing on things."

The reality of her situation hit home and panic slithered along her veins. She'd really, truly, holy shit-ly be giving up her life for these two men. Fear and excitement fought, and she wasn't sure which emotion was winning. At the moment, it resembled an even tie.

She ignored their expressions, the difference between the two easily visible. Keller's sadness and regret. Madden's hunger for her and confusion. She was going to have her hands full with these two.

Pretending they weren't tearing her apart with the upheaval of her life, she turned to the table and peeked beneath the covers. She set aside the metal domes as plate after plate of food was revealed. Steaks, salads and sides covered every inch along with a note indicating dessert could be found on a shelf below the tabletop. Yum.

The rustle of cloth told her that the men had decided to get up, but she kept her gaze averted. One look at their chiseled bodies and she'd be a goner, her snit forgotten. She padded toward a small seating area and snagged a chair. The wolf had placed their meal before a set of club chairs, and she decided her mates could take those while she remained opposite them. If she got within touching distance, they'd take control, and all she'd be able to think about was them claiming her.

Nope, they had issues to discuss. Their relationship and then… Whitney. And her cat.

Not necessarily in that order. Once they got onto discussing their mating, it'd probably go downhill and end in bed.

Right, Whitney first.

Scarlet settled into her straight-backed seat and waited, noting the pause in the rustle coming from behind her, but her wolves soon appeared.

Both men shot her longing looks but eased into their chairs. She noted they wore boxers. Well, at least she'd only be tempted by their chests.

"Um…" Madden cleared his throat.

Scarlet cut into her steak. Medium-rare. Perfect.

"Uh…" Keller looked so uncomfortable. Poor guy.

She popped a hunk of beef into her mouth and moaned around the bite. It melted like butter over her tongue. A glance from beneath her lashes showed that both of her mates' gazes were intent on her mouth.

"So, you're, uh, an administrative assistant? How long have you been doing that?" Madden's voice was strangled, as if he could barely breathe.

"Since college." She shrugged. "I'll be honest, I was pissed you guys haven't even stopped to get to know me. I mean, I know we're mates. I get it. But I don't even know your middle names or favorite color. Where do you live? When were you going to tell me you're the Ruling Alphas?" She closed her eyes and took a deep breath. "Being Marked is… It's hard. I've had this thing since I was born, and it meant my life was always in limbo. I went to college, but I rushed because I wasn't sure when I'd meet my mates and even if they'd let me finish and get my degree. I didn't know when I'd have to move. Where I'd have to go."

She sought to calm her ragged nerves. "I've lived for thirty years, waiting for the other shoe to drop. Gabby is the same way, but at least her job allows her to telecommute. Plus, there was the fear of dealing with two men, two wolves, for the rest of my life. I never went looking for my mates simply because I was scared. I wasn't looking forward to mating. Why do you think I've never attended a Gathering? And don't get me started on Whitney. Your witches got her *all* wrong."

Keller frowned. "I never realized. I mean, we never actually thought about what it'd be like for the women." He shook his head. "Your life had to be a shade of hell, Scarlet."

She shrugged, unwilling to wallow in her pity party. "No worse than any other Marked's I suppose. It sucks, but it is what it is."

Madden piped up. "No, it doesn't have to be. The urge to mate is intense, I admit that, but we can work together to make the transition easier."

Scarlet held up her hand. "No, it's not horrible. When I met you, the Mark woke and let me know you belonged to me. By dinner," she blushed, heat surging to her cheeks, "I was, uh, ready to cement things. But encouraging wolves to be a little understanding would probably help things when it came to your mates. I'm not saying everyone's life is like mine. Hell, there are probably plenty of women who are eager to abandon everything in a blink for their mates. And then there are others who will have a hard time."

She thought of Whitney, her poor sister who'd gone through life wishing for a Mark only to have the world play some cosmic joke. "We need to talk about Whitney, too." Scarlet took another bite of her steak, suppressing the urge to groan at the taste. Her mates looked on edge already. "She doesn't have a Mark, but she was summoned to the Gathering. It's cruel. She worked through the disappointment and jealousy of Gabby and I having Marks while she didn't, and then she got that stupid letter. She can't mate a single wolf because they mate with other wolves, but she's not Marked for an Alpha pair either. And yet, she's here. *And* if those witches are somehow going to pair her with a pair, those men better be God's gift to wolves or I'll shoot them myself." She frowned to make sure they knew she was serious.

"Are you certain she doesn't have a Mark?" Keller's voice was low, soothing yet disbelieving.

"She's been my sister for thirty years and has spent all of them wishing she had a Mark like me and Gabby. She never gave up looking, hoping she'd be a late bloomer, even though they are on our skin from birth. We do everything together. Except this." She shuddered. "And I've seen more of Whitney's parts every year than I care to mention while she double checks to see if she has one."

Keller and Madden shared a look, and she sensed they were engaged in a mental conversation. She couldn't wait to share that with them, complete their mating and be able to have those intimate, private talks.

Madden turned back to her. "We don't use witches, we use Wardens. They're wolves, but…not. We'll talk with them when they arrive tomorrow. She'll need to be, uh, examined—"

"By a female wolf." That was non-negotiable. She wasn't about to let her sister be manhandled by some stranger.

Keller nodded. "Okay, a female wolf."

She relaxed, letting go of the tension she'd been carrying. "Good."

Madden reached across the table and covered her hand with his, giving it a gentle squeeze. "We're mates, Scarlet. Probably not very good ones so far, but we want to do everything we can to make you happy. That includes taking care of your family. They belong to us, just as you do."

Some of the tension she'd been carrying dissipated. She recognized the truth in his words and relaxed. They could do this. Would do this.

Keller mirrored his partner's position, tugging her fork free and twining their fingers together. "And we'll work on merging our lives. *Merging,* not taking over. Your happiness is more important than anything. Ever."

63

Oh. Oh, wow. It was more than she'd hoped for when she thought of mating and this…

"Okay."

"Okay?" Hope sparkled in Madden's eyes.

She took a deep breath. "Yeah, okay."

"Good."

"What about my cat?"

Madden rolled his eyes. "We promise not to eat the spawn of Satan."

She snorted but nodded. "Good."

Keller gave her a wicked, wicked smile. "Now, I vote we finish our conversation in bed."

Butterflies took up residence in her stomach, but she allowed the men to lead her from the table, dismissing their half-finished meals. In a handful of steps, they were before the massive bed, and her mates urged her onto the soft mattress.

They settled on each side of her, both wolves staring down at her as if she were the tastiest treat. Heat unfurled in her belly, slinking along her nerves and warming her. She squirmed, working to alleviate the sudden ache between her thighs.

Madden, the more aggressive of her mates, leaned down and brushed a gentle kiss across her lips. When he pulled away, she followed him, raising and chasing that mouth.

A cocky chuckle was his only response. "Not yet, sweet. We need to get you naked first."

A sliver of unease stole into her.

"Hey, none of that." Keller nuzzled her. "I don't know why you're worried, but you are the most beautiful." Kiss. "Delectable—"

"Fuckable?" Madden's voice filled her other ear, and she heard Keller's growl.

Suddenly their heat left her, and her two mates glared at each other.

"What? It's true." The wolf looked so disgruntled that she reached up and stroked his shoulder, noting the heat of his skin beneath her fingertips.

"Thank you, Madden."

That earned her a small smile. Poor big, gruff guy. Keller seemed to be the charmer of the two, leaving her growly mate to stumble along in his wake. She'd have to be sure to show the man how much he meant to her, rough edges and all.

She let her hand travel north, digits slinking into the hair at the base of Madden's skull, and she tugged him back to her. She urged him closer, pulled until his lips were against hers.

Then it became his show. He growled and slipped his tongue into her mouth, licking and lapping at her. Flavors filled her, and she sought out more of his taste, searched for the essence of her heated mate. Moaning against his invasion, she suckled him and swallowed his groan.

They mimicked what was to come: the thrust and retreat of a seductive dance. His kiss alone aroused her, and then hands became involved.

Beneath Madden's assault, Keller's palms slid over her thighs, fingers hooking into the waist of her boxers. The room's cold air assailed her, stroked her exposed body.

"So pretty." Keller stroked her legs, dancing from hips to knees and back again, urging her to part her thighs. When had he moved? "So fucking gorgeous. You should see her pussy, Madden." A rough cheek scraped her inner thigh. "All wet and pink for us."

His words, more than his touch, aroused her further. Warm puffs of air bathed the juncture of her thighs, his heat adding to the desperate burn of her cunt. Her hips twitched and jerked of their own volition, searching out his touch.

A low chuckle came from between her legs, but she didn't have a moment to dwell on the sound.

No, not when Madden's hand was playing over her stomach, slipping beneath her shirt and dragging the material higher. He kept moving, exposing her until he cupped her breast.

Oh God, skin against skin was heaven. He palmed her mound, kneaded and rubbed her flesh, plucked her nipples. Shit. Fuck. It felt good. More than good. Paradise, and it was only foreplay.

She moaned into Madden's mouth. Her fingers were still tangled in his silken hair, and she tightened her grip.

Her low moan turned into something louder, harsher and soul deep.

Keller licked her pussy. His cheek resting against her thigh, while his tongue snaked out and lapped at her wet heat. It wasn't a tentative touch. No, he delved between her folds and moaned when the first hint of her cream coated his tongue.

Scarlet reached down and cupped his head, needing that connection as he pleasured her.

He went back again and again, his tongue doing wicked things to her pussy, tracing the center of her heat and flicking against her throbbing clit.

She gasped and groaned against Madden, unable to breathe, but unwilling to release him yet. He continued teasing her breasts, pinching her nipples, and the tiny sting added to the pleasure Keller created between her spread thighs.

Then Madden's lips were gone, tongue retreating. He pressed his forehead against hers and breathed into her mouth. "Is he good, sweet? Is he eating that hot little cunt?"

She whimpered, pussy clenching in response to his dirty talk.

"Oh, damn man, she likes that. She fucking coated my tongue." Keller's words barely registered over the thundering of her heart.

The wolf between her thighs went back to work, licking her in long strokes from hole to the top of her slit and back again.

"Fuck…"

Madden's eyes danced with mirth. "We'll get there, sweet. You need to come first. Then we'll stretch that pretty ass and both of us will fill you."

"Yes," she hissed. Keller latched onto her clit, tongue working the nub as he sucked on the bundle of nerves.

"Let's see how you like these little nipples sucked, hmm?" Madden leaned down and captured a single hard nubbin with his lips. He suckled the bit of flesh, alternating flicks and nibbles. Each pull went straight to her pussy, wrapping around her clit and stroking her from inside out.

She gasped and writhed, fighting to get closer, take more of what they offered. She was torn between the two men, the sensations they caused so different yet so similar.

Madden was take-charge, dominating her with his intensity. Meanwhile Keller was more seductive, coaxing responses from her in a slow beckoning.

But it all rolled together, coalesced and covered her in a rolling wave of pleasure.

Scarlet rocked against Keller, moving her hips and riding his talented mouth. Her nerves sang to her, shouting with the bubbles of ecstasy that slid through her with increasing frequency. She burned, blood heating with her increasing need until she felt like she'd burst into flames.

Madden abandoned one breast and she whined, distraught at the loss.

"No worries, sweet. We're gonna make you come."

"Please…" She wasn't above begging.

68

He went back to his ministrations, tongue taunting her, and somehow he picked up Keller's rhythm. They licked and sucked in time with each other, pushing her closer and closer to orgasm.

She tossed her head from side to side, unable to cope with the enormous pleasure they created.

Then—*holy shit*—they growled. The vibrations roared through her, the tiny bubbles of ecstasy suddenly blossoming into giant globes of sensation. They grew and grew, increasing in size until she couldn't think past the pleasure.

Tongues worked, licked and flicked. Teeth nibbled. Mouths sucked. And through it all she sobbed, begged and cried for her mates to end her torment.

It was all too much, so big and overwhelming. She no longer eased toward the edge of release but was tossed to the precipice. She teetered on the brink, wavering and then…

Keller threw her off, shoved her into the air with a scrape of his fang over her sensitive clit. The growing pleasure shattered into a thousand pieces. She screamed, roared as her release rolled through her.

Her Mark burned, the soul-searing heat enhancing her bliss until she wasn't sure where her body ended and her mates' began. Their consciousness eased closer, edging toward their joining, and she captured hints of their emotions.

Care… Affection… Need… And then…she shied away from that last feeling, unsure if she was ready to face it all.

Everything gathered and merged the pleasure boiling inside her, and just as quickly as it rose, it eased. In increments, her mates brought her floating back to her body. Tongues slowed, suction eased, and the orgasmic growls lessened until it sounded like they purred against her flesh.

"We're far from kittens, sweet." Madden nibbled her breast.

"But if it means you screaming for us again, we'll definitely try." Keller sounded way too smug.

They'd picked up on her thoughts, another signal their bond had grown.

She caught their words and her face burned. "I did scream, didn't I?"

Keller slithered up her body, his hardness rubbing along her leg and then resting on her hip. He kissed her, and she tasted the salty tang of her musk, the mixture of their flavors, and she didn't hesitate to accept his affections. There was something erotic about sharing their essences after he'd licked her to orgasm. And that something brought her arousal back to life.

Their tangle of tongues remained gentle, savoring, until he eased their kiss. Now she was faced with two horny, hotter than hell wolves.

And they wanted her.

\*

*Fuck.* Madden wanted her, wanted to sink deep into her pussy and fill her with his cum. He could sense her emotions, her thoughts, as they wafted over him. She ached for them, but was scared.

70

No, worried. Anxious. Something about…

"Your body is gorgeous, sweet mate. Luscious. Perfect for us." Keller got the jump on him. Fucker always did that.

A little of her wariness left her features, but he couldn't hold his words at bay. "Baby, if I don't get inside this pretty cunt, I'm gonna explode." His cock throbbed in agreement. "Fuck, wanna squeeze that ass while you ride me. Suck on your tits. Do you know how much I love them? All big and lush for us. Love 'em."

Fuck, fuck, fuck… He did.

Another hint of her cream drifted to him and he smiled, feeling more than a little smug. Yeah, his partner had the right words, but he had the naughty ones.

Madden couldn't get enough of looking at her, watching the rise and fall of her chest, the jiggle of those fucking awesome breasts. He loved the little curve of her belly, and he imagined her swollen with their cubs, big and round. *Fuck.* Those hips. Yeah, he ached to grab those hips while he pounded into her from behind, fantasized about how he'd spank her ass, get her all pink for them.

His dick throbbed, twitching within his boxers. Without taking his eyes from her, he reached down and thumped his erection, pushing back the need to come.

Couldn't. Not yet. Not until they were both balls deep inside their mate.

"You ready to be ours, Scarlet?" Keller traced her jaw, and those pretty chocolate eyes darkened.

Sometimes it paid to have someone else living in his head.

His shoulder burned, throbbed in time with his heart, and he knew he'd find her Mark in the same place on her body. That one spot connected them, signified their initial link.

She writhed, her plump body shifting between them. "Please."

His cock surged back to life, quickly recovering from his assault. He didn't bother flicking himself again. Not when his mate was so willing.

*Now?* He couldn't help sounding like a new pup.

*Now.* Keller's voice rang with satisfaction.

With similar movements, they stripped off their boxers. Scarlet's eyes darkened further. She licked her lips and the distinct urge to suck cock filled him.

Thankfully, it wasn't the need to get down and dirty with Keller. It was more along the lines of his mate sucking him down.

Madden reached down and encircled his dick, pumping his length. "Not yet, sweet. We get to fuck you first. Claim our fuckable mate."

She moaned, eyes drifting closed. "Madden."

"Come ride me, sweet." He rolled to his back, and Keller nudged her until she crawled atop Madden. "Slide onto my dick and then your mate is gonna open that luscious ass." A shudder overtook her. "Like that idea? Want Keller inside your ass? You're a dirty girl aren't you?"

Scarlet's eyes were nearly black with arousal, her pussy leaking more and more of that musky cream. She shifted, bringing her soaking cunt over his cock, and rocked against his length. Wet heat bathed his shaft, and he pushed his wolf back. The beast wanted out, wanted to sink his teeth into her vulnerable flesh and claim her.

Easy, Madden.

Easy? He almost snorted. Keller wasn't the one who had her pussy spread over his dick.

He encouraged Scarlet to rock against him, slide her scorching wetness along his shaft. Pleasure emanated from their point of contact, sending bolts of ecstasy through him. The bliss settled in his balls and made his prick twitch.

"Want you, Madden." She buried her face against his neck, and he felt the heat of her blush.

Madden gripped her hips, pushing and nudging until she was positioned as he desired. Her pussy kissed the head of his cock, suckling the spongy tip. "That what you need?"

Scarlet nodded, the warmth from her cheeks growing.

*Poor, sweet, needy mate.* Madden purred within his mind.

Her body was his to mold, move as he craved, and he took advantage of her gift.

Madden grit his teeth, gripped her hips and slowly lowered his lush mate's pussy along his dick.

"Shit, fuck." Moist silken heat surrounded him, squeezing and caressing his cock the deeper he sank into her pussy. Her walls grabbed his shaft, stroking and embracing him.

He sank deeper and deeper into her depths, her cunt swallowing him down. The further he traveled, the harder she squeezed him, her sheath rippling around his invasion. "Damn, sweet. So fucking tight."

Scarlet wiggled and he stilled her, drawing a whine from his little mate's lips. "Madden."

"Tell me, sweet." He flexed his hips, pushing deeper into her cunt.

"Burns. S'good."

"Yeah?" The soft click of a bottle being opened reminded him of Keller's presence. "Ready for more, Scarlet? Keller wants your ass. He's gonna stretch you, and he'll sink balls deep into your hole. Want that?"

Her pussy tightened around him as shudders wracked her body. A soft moan reached his ears.

"Yeah, you want it." He couldn't hold back his smug smile. "Ride me now. It'll make it so much better, sweet. Get you all hot. I'm filling your needy cunt, and he'll play with your hungry ass."

*"Madden."* She admonished him, but did as he asked.

Scarlet moved, a slight slither up his cock and back down again, her walls clinging to him with her tiny bit of progress. It didn't matter how small her shift, his dick twitched and throbbed within her. His balls drew high and tight, begging for permission to come inside his mate.

"Fuck." A growl rolled through him and his mate squeaked, pussy clamping down on his prick.

She gave another squeak for an altogether different reason. "Keller."

Madden raised his head and looked over Scarlet's shoulder to find his partner kneeling between his and Scarlet's spread thighs, Keller's focus entirely on their mate's ass. Beneath his gaze, Keller reached for her back entrance. From then on, he couldn't see what the other wolf was doing to their little human. But whatever it was, she loved every moment.

Scarlet's previously timid tempo increased, became more forceful as she rode his cock. Her pussy clasped his dick like a wet fist, and he went along for the journey.

"Keller. Madden. Oh, God."

"Tell me, Scarlet."

She whimpered and shivered, but did as he asked. Her walls spasmed, and he smiled. Oh yeah, his sweet liked dirty talk.

"Burns. But feels so good." She scraped her teeth along his neck, and he nearly came. A shooting pulse of ecstasy overtook him, and he fought back the need to fill her with his seed.

"What's he doing to you?" He couldn't wait until he and his partner could swap positions. It wouldn't happen the first time around. Madden was thicker than Keller, and they didn't want to risk hurting her during the frenzy of their mating.

"He's... His finger is in my ass." A low whine. "More now. He's got them *there*."

Yeah, Madden just bet. Keller's invasion increased the pressure and tightness of Scarlet's cunt. Damn, he loved it when they took a woman together. The heat. The fierce squeeze.

But it'd never be anyone but Scarlet now. Not that he cared. No one was as perfect as their little human.

"Shit, shit, shit." Scarlet chanted breathlessly.

The pressure increased. "More, sweet? Tell me."

"More, more, more. He's fucking my ass with his fingers, Madden. It's so hot. Burns. Want more." Scarlet's tempo took on a desperate edge, pussy stroking his dick with every rise and fall, urging him toward release.

*Hold it, fucker.* Keller's mental voice sounded more wolf than man.

With each additional finger, she grew tighter, squeezing him almost the point of pain. But fuck, it was worth it. Their mate tossed any inhibitions aside and took what she wanted, used their bodies as she desired.

*"Nooo..."* She pushed back hard, slamming her hips down and he groaned. The increased pressure at the base of his cock was nearly his undoing. He loved intense compression near the root, and his mate had given what he treasured

most. "He took it away. Give it back. Madden, tell him to fuck my ass."

Madden wrapped his arms around her and stroked her back, soothing her. "Easy, he's gonna. He'll give you what you need."

"Mad— Oh." The ferocious pressure returned, more than before, and he groaned. Finally. Finally he'd get to come inside his mate and claim her.

We.

Right. We.

He'd get that right. Eventually. But fuck if he cared when Scarlet knotted around his cock.

*

"Scarlet."

She wiggled, pushing back against his hint of invasion.

"Scarlet, don't move, damn it."

She didn't listen. Part of Keller hated that the woman couldn't take direction to save her life. His cock was fucking grateful as hell. Careful of her tight asshole, he eased forward, shuddering at the snug warmth that bathed his dick.

Deeper and deeper he sank, just a small bit of tissue separating his shaft from Madden's. He practically felt the ridges along the other man's length. His partner's presence made everything that much better. It increased the pressure and forced their mate to hold them like a clenched fist.

His possession solidified the rightness of their situation, made every breath perfect.

He pressed into her forbidden hole, more and more of him disappearing into Scarlet. Her mewls and whines spurred his need, pushed him closer to the edge of release.

Keller's cock had throbbed and twitched throughout her preparation. He'd sunk one finger, then two, and finally three into her ass. She'd begged for more the entire time.

Yeah, she was perfect for them.

Now, they'd claim her as theirs.

His journey continued, their sweet mate babbling every moment.

"So deep. He's inside my asshole. Madden, Keller's fucking me." Her voice was a high alto, rising above their deep groans.

"Take it, sweet." Madden encouraged their mate, and Keller was thankful for his partner.

Keller couldn't speak. Not when he finally bottomed out inside her, his hips meeting the flesh of her plump ass. Fuck. They were in. And so close to their claiming.

In.

"Gonna move, Scarlet."

"Yes, yes, yes…"

Keller's world was reduced to sensation. The drag of his dick as he slid in and out of her fist-like hole. The heat that assaulted him with every move. The way she clenched and spasmed when Madden pushed deep. She'd relax for a breath before the pulses came again.

Their bodies moved in counterpoint. Madden pushed in as Keller retreated, alternating their thrusts.

Scarlet was immobile between them, mewling, whining and groaning as they made love to their woman.

He pushed in and withdrew again, savoring the slick drag of her tight hole against his cock. *God, yes.* She milked him, them, in rapid succession.

Pleasure wrapped around his dick, slithered down and cupped his balls. The spasms groped him, reached into his body and tugged him closer to release.

Keller's growls and groans joined Madden's. Their sounds intermingled with Scarlet's until their world was a rolling bundle of sexual music. The pace increased, he and Madden upping the rhythm in sync.

Sweat gathered on his skin, the salty wetness helping cool him as they all struggled toward the pinnacle. Droplets slid from his temples and along his cheeks to fall onto his mate's creamy skin.

The heated musk of their sex filled the air, the scent adding to his wolf's delirious need. His teeth ached, a stinging filling his gums as his fangs pierced the flesh. The beast demanded he sink his teeth into Scarlet's shoulder.

Her left shoulder for him and her right for Madden. The marks would join them to her. For life.

"Harder. Please." Scarlet's voice was barely a whisper, the words released with a low sob.

Keller couldn't deny her. No, he increased the power behind his next thrust, shaking the bed. Out. *Fuck, s'good.* In.

His body slammed into hers, Madden echoing his force. The bedframe trembled, giving them a wordless warning.

Yeah, they'd probably break the thing.

He didn't care. Not when his mate begged and pleaded, asking for more. His main goal was to please her. Always.

Right now, he needed her to come, her orgasm giving them permission to do the same.

Keller plunged in and out, the lewd slap of bodies and wet squishing of their coming together joining their moans and growls. The sounds added to the pleasure, added to the wicked thrill of sharing their mate.

The tingling surrounding his cock and balls intensified, burgeoning until it encompassed his body. "Fuck. Need to come, sweet. Give it to us."

He shoved his orgasm back, refusing to finish without his mate and partner.

"Yes, yes, yes…" The rhythmic spasms upped in pace until she rippled around him in an ever increasing beat. "Gonna…"

Keller let go, releasing his control, and his wolf seized power. Beast in command, he leaned forward. Madden's wolfish gaze met his, and they were in accord.

Now.

As one, they opened their mouths and sank their fangs into Scarlet's shoulders, biting deep and scarring her for one and all to see.

His cock pulsed, twitching within her, and his climax roared through his body, pleasure slamming into him like a sledgehammer.

She was theirs.

*

Scarlet's scream echoed in the room, the pleasure of their possession warring with the fierce pain of their bites, and she was overwhelmed with the sensations. Ecstasy raced in a circle, bouncing from body to body, and a rush of emotions assaulted her. Words, flashes of thoughts and desires pummeled her mind.

She sorted through them as she traveled along the never-ending trail of bliss that connected their souls. Their bodies were frozen still while their mating links fell into place, locking them in an eternal embrace.

She fought for breath, fought to retain some semblance of self as her mate's thoughts battered her. They pushed against her mind and snuggled into corners she'd never known existed.

Inhale. Exhale. Struggle for control. This new connection finally settled, easing into a gentle flowing river instead of raging rapids. With every new heartbeat, the tornado of sensation eased. It continued its downward spiral until her mates' mental presence was nothing more than a lapping stroke amidst her thoughts.

First Keller and then Madden released her flesh, soothing her wounds with gentle strokes of their tongues until all pain left her.

"Wow." Scarlet was awed by the tumultuous pleasure and pain that came from their joining.

"Yeah." Keller sounded as if he felt the same.

"Fuck, man. Let's do it again." Madden's words caused Scarlet to grin against his neck, and she nuzzled him. She imagined he'd always be her crass, protective, adorable man.

"Damn straight." She chuckled, more than happy to "suffer" through their attentions once more.

Keller recovered first. "Easy, sweet. Sit still. I don't think you're ready for another round."

She pouted. "Are you sure?"

Madden's cock twitched, thickening within her pussy, and she winced. Her walls were raw and tingling in a not-fun way. "Yeah, we're sure."

Scarlet sighed but didn't argue. Yeah, banging needed to go on hiatus for a little while. Keller moved, withdrawing his cock from her ass, and she moaned at the loss.

"Shh… We'll do it again soon. Just maybe not today."

She kept her face buried against the wolf beneath her and nodded. When cool air hit her back, she shivered, a chill pushing through her. But she became warm again in moments. Madden eased her from him, slowly rolling her to his side and settling her between her two mates.

They bracketed her, holding her between them, and she realized they'd probably spend the rest of their lives like this.

She signed and let her eyes drift closed. "So, since I don't get any more lovin', someone wanna tell me why you guys share a room and a bed? I mean, there was no sword-crossing just now. But it's cool, you know, if you guys… I just wanna watch, m'kay?"

More growls. God, she loved their growls.

# EPILOGUE

Bleary, Scarlet wiped the sleep from her eyes and stumbled into the main area of the suite. She chose to ignore the massive array of guards positioned throughout the room. She also decided to pretend none of them heard her during the previous night with Keller and Madden.

Keep dreaming, sweet.

She mentally harrumphed at Keller. Damn man needed to leave her to her delusions.

So, telling you they were all jealous they weren't the ones buried in your delicious cunt would be a bad thing? She could "hear" the smile in Madden's voice.

This time, she growled.

The jerks laughed.

Double jerks.

Scarlet shuffled toward the center of the room, knowing without a doubt that her sisters would come hunting her. At least she could order room service before they sniffed her out like bloodhounds.

It took mere moments to secure food, a lot of food, and she snuggled into a comfy chair to wait.

Thankfully, breakfast arrived before Gabby and Whitney. Marginally before, but she still had five minutes with a cup of coffee.

Gabby's yell reached her first, loud, but muffled. The elevator doors were still closed. Great. "You open these doors, or I'll bite you! I may not have furball teeth, but I can still break skin!"

Damn, the woman had a set of lungs on her.

Scarlet glanced around the space and found a familiar guard. "Can you tell them to let my sisters in? They're not going to kill me. At least, not without a lot of effort, and you can save me before things get bloody."

The wolf grinned and left the room, presumably to do as she asked. When the yells got louder, she realized he'd followed through. Well, that was pretty cool. She got to tell people what to do, and they *listened*.

She wondered if that'd work on Keller and Madden.

*Not on your life.* Keller's mental voice held a growl.

*Only if I get a blow job first.* Ah, Madden, her practical man.

Stomps from the entryway grew louder, and her sisters burst into the room.

"Coffee?" Yeah, Gabby wasn't a morning person without coffee.

*"Breakfast."* Whitney shared her love of nummies.

"Ooh, Danishes." Gabs eyed the apple-filled treats.

"And chocolate muffins. I love you." Yeah, that was Whitney. She was a sucker for chocolate.

Gabby's eyes drifted closed the moment her lips touched the mug. Scarlet smiled, sad this would be ending. No more morning munchies and getting together for no reason other than the fact that they were sisters. They probably wouldn't live fifteen minutes from each other, like they were used to, when all was said and done.

*Not for forever, sweet. We'll figure things out.* Keller's voice held a hint of the sadness that inched into her heart.

*I'm fine.* She wasn't, but she could pretend.

The Captain of the guard came into the room, giving her a jerky nod, and then he froze, hand going to his arm.

She furrowed her brow. "Captain?" Scarlet really needed to learn the man's real name. She refused to wander around calling the wolf by his title for all eternity.

*You will.*

Scarlet mentally snorted. *Not.*

Brushing her mate's grumbles aside, she returned her focus to the statue-like guard. "You okay?" The man's eyes were glowing bright, edging closer and closer to pure yellow. "Captain?"

Real worry assaulted her, but then her mates entered, half-clothed, and rushed toward the Captain. A few low words were exchanged, and Keller and Madden lead him away. Every few steps, the agitated wolf looked back, seeming to strain against her mate's hold.

Returning her attention to her sisters, she noticed Gabby's focus was on the wolf while she rubbed her left bicep. "Gabs?"

"Huh, what?" Gabby shook her head. "Sorry, did you say something?"

She eyed her sister, wishing the three of them shared the same type of connection she had with her mates. "No. So, either of you find Misters Wonderful?"

Gabby looked toward the doorway where Scarlet's mates and the Captain had disappeared, then back at Scarlet. "No. But it's only Saturday morning. We've got a few more days, right?"

"Uh huh." She didn't believe those words for a second. *"Right."*

"Whatever." Her sister pegged her with a strawberry. "So, I figured you did the mating thing last night, I can grab a pair today, and we'll sort out Whitney. Get this shit wrapped in time for our flight on Sunday."

Whitney tossed a grape at Gabby. "Crass much?" She popped a piece of fruit into her mouth. "So, how's mating?"

Scarlet thought about it for a minute, replayed their night of lovemaking, kissing and caressing and coming... "Squishy."

A sense of male satisfaction crept into her mind, and her clit twitched. Yeah, she could deal with squishy for a long, long, lemme-come-some-more time.

# THE END

If you enjoyed Scarlet, please be totally awesomesauce and leave a review so others may discover it as well. Long review or short, your opinion will help other readers make future purchasing decisions. So, go forth and rate my level-o-awesome!

By the way… you can check at the rest of the Alpha Marked series on Celia's website: http://celiakyle.com/alphamarked

# About Celia Kyle

Ex-dance teacher, former accountant and erstwhile collectible doll salesperson, New York Times and USA Today bestselling author Celia Kyle now writes paranormal romances for readers who:

1) Like super hunky heroes (they generally get furry)
2) Dig beautiful women (who have a few more curves than the average lady)
3) Love laughing in (and out of) bed.

It goes without saying that there's always a happily-ever-after for her characters, even if there are a few road bumps along the way.

Today she lives in Central Florida and writes full-time with the support of her loving husband and two finicky cats.

If you'd like to be notified of new releases, special sales, and get FREE eBooks, subscribe here:
http://celiakyle.com/news

You can find Celia online at:
http://celiakyle.com
http://facebook.com/authorceliakyle
http://twitter.com/celiakyle

# COPYRIGHT PAGE

CPSIA information can be obtained
at www.ICGtesting.com
Printed in the USA
LVHW111749240119
605131LV00003B/581/P